Silly YaYa

Story and Illustrations by
Violet Favero

I dedicate this book to my grandchildren; who inspired me to write this story.

A special thank you to my son, Matthew Favero, for being my graphic editor and illustration advisor. I could not have done this without your design guidance, encouragement and belief that I could, indeed, illustrate this book.

Barbara Leek, thank you for your outstanding editing and patience.

ISBN-10: 1512133000

ISBN-13: 978-1512133004

Illustrations rendered with colored pencil and ink.

Printed by CreateSpace, An Amazon.com Company

First Printing 2015

My name is Yaya.
It's silly you see, but it's the name my
grandchildren gave me.

Your mommy and daddy
have a mommy and daddy too.
They are your grandparents
and they love you.

When you were
a baby and you
couldn't yet
walk, you learned
what to call your
grandparents'
before you
could talk.

Some children have
lots of grandparents.
How about you?
Maybe you have
just one, or
maybe a few.

Each one needs their own special name.

Ema

Gigi

Minnie

Skip

From family to family, they are not always the same.

Sometimes the names we call
them come from a
place far away,

Nonna

Oma & Opa

Zu Ma & Zu Fu

Avozinha & Avozinho

Grand Mere & Grand-Pere

Savta & Zayde

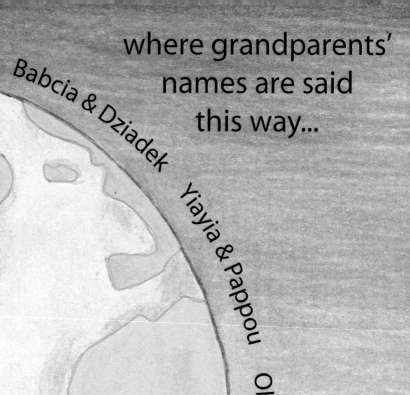

where grandparents'
names are said
this way...

Nonno

Babcia & Dziadek

Yiayia & Pappou

Obaason & Ojiisan

Mormor & Morfar

Abuela & Abuel...

Sometimes the name you call them isn't what your parents told you at all. Maybe you made it up, or it was a sound you made when you were just small.

Sometimes we spell it a little silly you see, but it's okay to be silly in this spelling bee.

Whatever you call them,
your grandparents
love you so much.

They love it when you
visit, and sit on their lap.
Sometimes, you even get
to skip your nap!

When you're with them
you get to do so many things,
like go to the park,

or eat popcorn
while watching a
movie in the dark:

or maybe they take you to the
playground and push you on a swing,

or read you stories,
where the endings
have a zing,

or maybe they pull you
in a wagon, and your
Teddy Bear gets to go too,

or sometimes they
take you to feed the
elephants at the zoo.

When it is sunny and
warm outside, you get
to build a sand
castle at the beach,

or they help you climb a tree,
when a branch is out of reach,

or they teach you
to fish, when no
fish are in sight,

or they take you to
fly a kite. It's so much
fun, and you squeal
with delight,

They love it when
you run up to them
and hug them tight.

So squeeze them hard
with all your might.

Did this book show the grandparents' names that you know?

Whether
yes or no,
please write
them below.

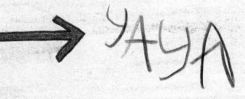

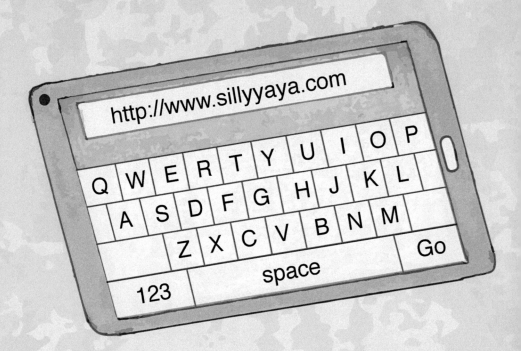

Follow Me Online

Made in the USA
San Bernardino, CA
04 July 2017